Jamela

Jamela

Jamela

Jamela

Jamela

For the brave children of the
Red Cross Hospital School,
Cape Town

Copyright © 2004 by Niki Daly / By arrangement with The
Inkman, Cape Town, South Africa / Hand-lettering by
Andrew van der Merwe / All rights reserved / First published
in Great Britain by Frances Lincoln Limited, 2004 / Printed
and bound in Singapore / First American edition, 2004
10 9 8 7 6 5 4 3 2 1

www.fsgkidsbooks.com

Library of Congress Cataloging-in-Publication Data
Daly, Niki.
     Where's Jamela? / story & pictures by Niki Daly. — 1st
American ed.
        p. cm.
     Summary: When Mama gets a new job and a new house,
everyone is excited about moving except Jamela who likes
her old house just fine.
     ISBN 0-374-38324-3
     [1. Moving, Household—Fiction.   2. Change—Fiction.
3. Blacks—South Africa—Fiction.   4. South Africa—
Fiction.]   I. Title: Where's Jamela?.   II. Title.

PZ7.D1715Wj 2004
[E]—dc22
                                                                2003049485

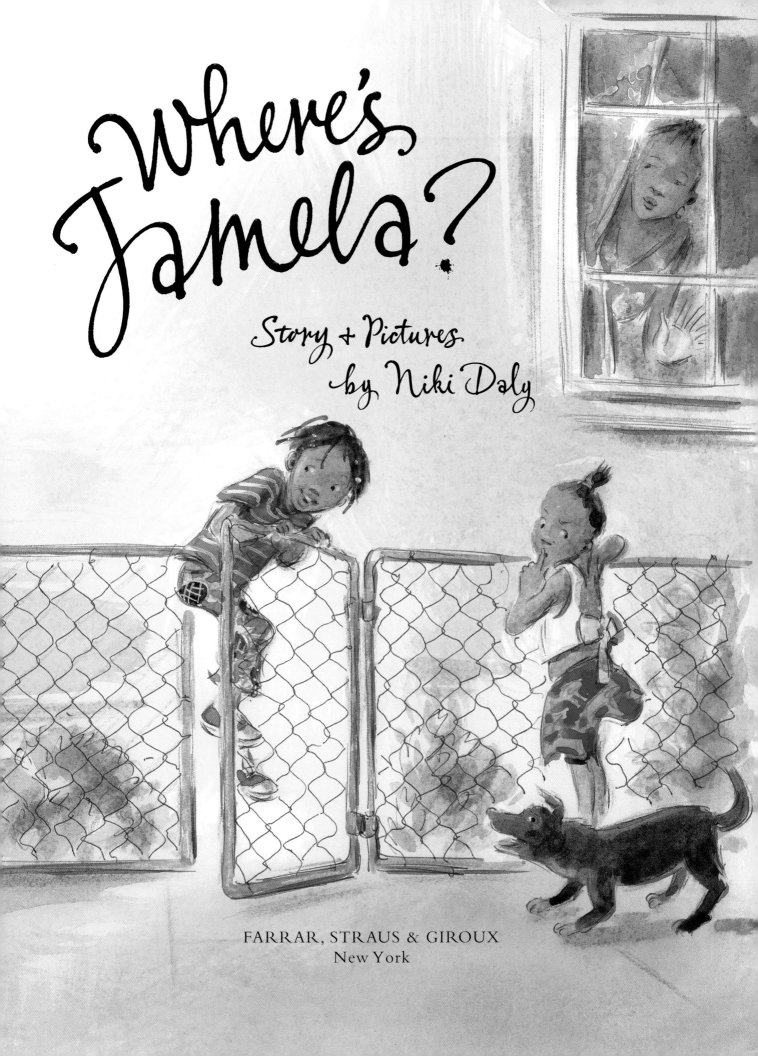

Where's Jamela?

Story + Pictures
by Niki Daly

FARRAR, STRAUS & GIROUX
New York

"I've got it! I've got it!" sang Jamela's mama as she danced around the kitchen table, clutching a letter.

"What have you got, Mama?" asked Jamela.

"A new job and a new place to stay," said Mama. "Oh, Jamela, we are going to be very happy in our new house."

"But I like this one, Mama," Jamela said, frowning.

"You will *love* the new house," said Mama. "There's a nice room for you and one for Gogo, if she'd like to stay with us."

Jamela wasn't happy about Mama's plans. She loved their old house with its squeaky front gate to swing on. She loved her bedroom window and the world she saw out of it. She loved the street sounds—Greasy Hands revving up old cars, Mrs. Zibi shouting at her chickens, dogs barking, and children playing. At suppertime, there was always a nice smell of cooking.

And high above, in the evening sky, a star looked down
on Jamela as she lay in bed.

A few days later, Gogo came around with her bags. She said it would be lovely to move in with Mama and Jamela, as long as they could bring the old piano.

"No problem," said Mama. "Greasy Hands is coming this afternoon with a big truck to move everything."

Mama and Gogo chatted about Mama's new job and the new house and how happy they were all going to be. Jamela didn't like all the talk about new things.

When Gogo saw how unhappy Jamela looked, she smiled and said, "Come, Jamela, you can help me pack."

Jamela started wrapping the teapot, but it got all twisted up in newspaper. Suddenly it fell right out of her hands and crashed onto the floor.

"Oh, Jamela!" cried Mama. "That's my only teapot!"

Jamela felt terrible.

Gogo patted her and said quietly, "Why don't you go and pack your things, sweetie?"

Jamela put Christmas, her chicken, into the special cage
that Mrs. Zibi had given her for the move.

Then she carefully wrapped
her pink butterfly tea set
in toilet paper so that
nothing would break.

She packed it safely
into her little
red suitcase.

Mama brought a big cardboard box and wrote on it

Jamela's Box

Jamela packed her red suitcase into the box, then her books, then her dolls, and finally all her school things.

By now Jamela was fed up with packing. There was too much thumping, bumping, and fussing going on around her.

So she climbed into the box, pulled down the flaps, and packed herself away.

Soon she
was fast asleep.

Meanwhile, Greasy Hands and his friend Lucky
turned up and started carrying all the boxes, bags,
and suitcases out to the truck.

"Be careful with my precious things," said Mama.
"Don't scratch my piano!" cried Gogo.
"Don't worry—be happy!" joked Greasy Hands.

After a lot of hard work, the truck was almost loaded.
"Don't forget this one, Greasy Hands," said Gogo.
Greasy Hands lifted the box and carried it
carefully to the truck.

"Be careful!" said Mama, as Greasy Hands passed the big box to Lucky.

"*Yebo!*" said Lucky. "I know— it's precious!"

Then they were ready to go. Gogo sat in the front
with Greasy Hands, while Mama and Lucky sat on boxes
at the back of the truck.

"Hold on tight!" called Greasy Hands, as he started
the truck.

But before they could move off, Mama shouted,
"Wait, wait! Where's Jamela?"

Everyone rushed back into the house. Mama called loudly, "Jamela! Jamela!" They looked in every room.

"Maybe she's run away," said Gogo. "She was very unhappy about us moving to a new house." "Oh, Gogo, do you think so?" said Mama. She looked very worried.

Mama and Gogo ran down the road. At Miss Style hairdressers, they asked the ladies, "Have you seen Jamela?"

"No," said the ladies. "What's up?"

Next they asked Mrs. Zibi, "Have you seen Jamela?"

"No!" said Mrs. Zibi. "Is Jamela up to her tricks again?"

Meanwhile, Greasy Hands called the police. When Mama and Gogo returned to the truck, a sergeant was busy taking down a description of Jamela.

"She's about six years old. She's wearing funky trousers and sporty red shoes. She's got beaded braids. She's a really cool kid," explained Greasy Hands.

The sergeant looked up from his notebook, then grinned. "Like the one sitting in the box?" he said, pointing with his pen.

They all turned around . . .

. . . and there was Jamela—awake at last!

The neighbors cheered. Gogo was so happy that she climbed onto the truck, opened her piano, and started to play.

Everyone began to sing and dance. It was a going-away song.
Jamela could see tears in Mama's eyes. It was time to go.

Later that afternoon, the truck pulled up outside a little house
in the suburbs. Mama was right. It was a very nice house—
with a wooden door, two windows,
a curvy fence, and a front gate.

"Listen, Mama . . . it squeaks!"
squealed Jamela.

When everything was unloaded, everyone looked tired and hot.

"*Shu!*" said Gogo. "I'd love a cup of tea, but we don't have a teapot."

Jamela remembered the broken teapot. Suddenly she had an idea! She found her suitcase and took out her pink plastic tea set with the butterflies. Excitedly, she filled the teapot at the new kitchen sink.

Then she called, "Mama! Gogo! Everyone! Come and have some tea!"

Jamela poured and handed everyone a tiny cup.
"Thank you, Jamela," said Gogo. "This is just
what we needed."

That night, Jamela lay in bed looking out the window. Somewhere a meowing cat was driving some poor dog mad. There was a spicy smell coming from the Bombay Take-out. Across the road, *kwaito* music started to play. When Gogo and Mama came in to say good night, Gogo said, "*Shu*, this place is crazy with life."

"Well, it's home now, Ma," said Mama. "What do you think, Jamela?"

High above the rooftops, Jamela saw her little star in its right place up in the evening sky. She smiled and said, "I think it's going to be all right, Mama."

Mama kissed her good night. Gogo gave her a tickle. Then Jamela rolled over and went to sleep in her new room in her new home—under the same old sky.